IT'S A DOG'S LIFE

IT'S A DOG'S LIFE

The adventures of a Knightsbridge Poodle

Toffee Parker

Illustrated by Una-Mary Parker

Severn House

This first world edition published 2015
in Great Britain and in the USA by
SEVERN HOUSE PUBLISHERS LTD of
19 Cedar Road, Sutton, Surrey, England, SM2 5DA.
Trade paperback edition first published
in Great Britain and the USA 2015 by
SEVERN HOUSE PUBLISHERS LTD

British Library Cataloguing in Publication Data

Parker, Toffee (Dog) author.
  It's a dog's life.
  1. Toffee Parker (Dog)–Fiction. 2. Parker, Una-Mary–Fiction
  3. Human-animal relationships–Fiction.
  4. Knightsbridge (London, England)–Social life and
  customs–Fiction. 5. Autobiographical fiction.
  I. Title
  823.9'-dc23

ISBN-13: 978-0-7278-9196-9 (cased)
ISBN-13: 978-0-7278-9214-0 (e-book)

Typeset by Palimpsest Book Production Ltd.,
Falkirk, Stirlingshire, Scotland.
Printed digitally in the USA.

Contents

Introduction

The moment Toffee scampered into my house I realized she and I were going to have a bumpy ride. At eleven weeks her multifaceted personality was apparent. This was no little angel. Her determination to rule the roost was obvious, but she took control of our lives with such charm and cunning that I found myself laughing most of the time. One minute she'd throw a tantrum and the next she'd want a cuddle. Toffee was soon referred to by our neighbours as a 'Little Person'. She is my constant companion, which means there's never a dull moment. I am so proud of her for writing a book telling the story of the first ten years of her life, and she and I are so delighted that Severn House are publishing it.

The Day I Hit High Society

Did you say Dinner was ready?

Let me introduce myself. My name is Toffee, and I'm a dark chocolate-brown Miniature Poodle. Before you so rudely ask, I should think that it's perfectly clear that I'm a *girl*, and very sweet – at least I *look* sweet – but Una-Mary who lives with me, has, I admit, seen my darker side. When I was driven down from Shropshire, where I was born, to the smartest part of London, and ushered into an exquisite Georgian house with a garden, I just knew I'd landed *avec mon derrière dans le beurre*. U-M didn't look so bad either. I'd sat on her lap being as good as gold and I could tell she'd fallen for me.

'Isn't she adorable?' she'd crooned, enchanted. That's the effect I have on people.

'She's a menace,' John, my breeder's husband, had reported flatly. 'She howled for the first hour and a half of the journey.'

'Poor little thing. She was probably missing her mother,' she'd replied. I'd sneaked her my sad poor-little-me look whilst keeping an eye on some delicious-looking biscuits on the tea tray. It was obvious back then that we were going to get along like a house on fire, and it had taken me only two minutes to suss her out as a soft touch. She's been my companion for ten years now, and I think I've looked after her quite well.

U-M is a writer like me, though this is my first book, and we spend several hours every afternoon in what she calls 'the office', though it looks to me like a cosy, cluttered little room filled with books and paintings, photographs of her big family and a few pretty ornaments. Naturally I recline on a small sofa, and we often listen to classical music while she taps away on the keyboard. I'm quite a connoisseur of Rachmaninov piano concertos. Very conveniently for me, there is also a door that leads on to our paved garden. Well, you have to think about these things!

Life can be exciting and very social. The last dinner party U-M gave went on until five in the morning. God, was I tired and bored. Being in high society seems to be about being polite and charming and never making a puddle in public. I once made the mistake of assuming the blinis weren't *exclusively* for the grown-ups, and was treated like a pariah for the rest of the party. I wonder how the Queen's dogs manage to behave? I've heard there's blotting paper and a bottle of soda water in every room in Buckingham Palace, but U-M says that's just gossip.

My personal claim is that I have wonderful diagnostic skills, which is lucky because, for a start, I've been able to save U-M from going blind. As a writer, her eyesight is vital, but it took a while before she listened to me and did anything about it. I'd heard that dogs in America are trained to sniff out cancer, and doctors find this invaluable. We have a very powerful sense of smell, many thousands of times stronger than that of humans.

When something about U-M's eyes didn't seem right, I decided to examine her more closely. Frankly, my instincts had told me that something had suddenly gone wrong. Not that she seemed bothered. She plastered the eyeshadow and mascara on every morning without a care in the world.

I knew she'd had cataract operations several years ago and she'd been thrilled by the results. I also knew she went for an annual check-up and wasn't due to see the ophthalmic surgeon again for another six months.

I have to admit there was a certain amount of self-interest involved here. Supposing she lost her sight? She'd have to get a specially trained guide dog, and what would become of me? It didn't bear thinking about.

I had to get to work, and fast, so every morning I stood over her as she lay in bed and I examined each eye carefully and with great concentration, keeping just a whisker away as I sniffed and sniffed. Undoubtedly, whatever it was had affected her right eye more than her left.

'What are you doing, Toffee?' she'd ask, amused. This went on for several weeks.

'You funny girl,' she said one morning as she stroked my silky ears, while I examined her eyes with growing concern. 'What are you planning to do to me? Brain surgery? Or a facelift?'

I snorted with disgust at her frivolity and turned away. Something *was* wrong and all she could do was tease me. I had to make her understand, so I sat down and thought hard about it.

'Toffee, what is it?' she inquired. 'Why don't you go out on to the balcony and direct the traffic? You know you love doing that.'

She was right. I like to put my head through the curly wrought iron railings and bark like mad if a lorry tries to park right outside our house. Or a van. Or a flashy car with a revving engine. How dare they? This is a Regency square with a big garden in the middle. If I was a warden I'd only let horses and carriages come this way.

I glanced at U-M despairingly. I used to regard her as fairly intelligent. Now I wasn't so sure. The situation was getting very frustrating.

To let off steam I went over to my toy basket and, selecting a squeaky rubber bird, I endeavoured to kill it.

However, later that morning I heard her on the phone making an appointment with her eye surgeon's secretary. At last! I went over to her, hoping for a pat on the head. She not only stroked my coat but she gave me a dog biscuit as well. Wow! I was gratified that she'd finally listened to me.

When U-M returned from her appointment a few days later she looked fairly stunned and kept glancing at me with a puzzled expression.

'It's the most extraordinary thing . . .' I heard her say as she talked to her daughter, Baba, on her mobile. 'You know how Toffee has been sniffing my eyes every morning in a weird kind of way? Especially my right eye?'

I perked up and jumped on her lap to hear more.

'Apparently,' she continued, 'I've recently developed glaucoma. Yes. And it's especially bad in my right eye. How strange is that? What? Oh, oh, I've got to have eye drops and perhaps laser treatment to bring the pressure down but it's nothing to worry about because we've caught it in the early stages.'

I noted the 'we'. It was *me* who raised the alarm, thank you very much.

U-M stroked my ears and then I heard her say, 'I was asked why I'd gone back so soon after the last appointment.'

There was a pause, and then she started laughing.

'Well, I could hardly tell them my dog had sent me, could I?'

Learning about Una-Mary's past

I thought I was the model around here.

Shortly after my arrival in London, U-M produced some old scrapbooks to show to a journalist who was interviewing her for a magazine feature. Old being the operative word; the books, I mean, not the journalist and certainly not U-M! They contained cuttings and pictures from 1956. That's history!

'That year,' U-M began in a dreamy voice, 'my late husband, Archie, said the most wonderful thing to me and I'll never forget his words. They changed my life forever.'

I blushed under my curly coat. Wasn't I too young to be listening to such obviously intimate moments?

Even the journalist's eyes popped. 'Oh, yes?' she inquired brightly. 'And what was that?'

U-M smiled. 'He said—', and here she paused for dramatic effect. 'He said, "I think you should get a little dog".'

I nearly fell off the sofa, but not before detecting some disappointment in the journalist's expression.

'Really?' she replied, distinctively unenthusiastic.

U-M beamed. 'He suggested I get a Poodle.'

I wished I'd known him when I heard that. He was obviously a man with exquisite taste.

'Right. So tell me about your job as the social correspondent on *Queen* magazine before it became *Harper's & Queen*. Is it true you went to six parties a night?'

U-M wasn't listening. She was about to have one of her 'got-to-tell-you-all-about-it' moments. When that happens there's no stopping her, so it's best to just sit back and listen.

'All my life I'd wanted a dog,' she began, 'but every time I begged my family the answer was always *no*. Dogs, they said, were dirty, messy and a terrible tie. So I begged for a kitten but the answer was still no. I even wrote to Father Christmas every year, throwing my note on to the blazing coal fire, hoping the blackened fragments of paper that swirled up the chimney would reach him, but to no avail. *Then* I asked if I could have a rabbit. Or even a budgerigar. The answer was always the same. My family would welcome an animal in the house about as much as they would dry rot.'

U-M drew breath, shaking her head sadly while the journalist nodded with a glazed expression. But I was all ears. I wanted to hear more. I was also horrified that they didn't like dogs. Dirty and messy, indeed. I felt personally offended.

'The strange thing,' U-M continued, 'was that when my parents finally divorced when I was seventeen, Daddy went back to Scotland to breed Alsatians as guard dogs and my mother started breeding Scotties. She showed them at Crufts and was immensely proud when they won prizes. I think it must have been my grandmother, who lived with us and looked after me, who strongly objected to our having a pet. She was probably afraid she'd end up having to look after the dog as well as the baby! Then a few years later, my mother moved to a bigger house where she had a dressing room leading off her bedroom, and do you know what she turned it into?'

By now the journalist not only didn't care, she looked as if she'd lost the will to live. 'You went on to work at *Tatler* magazine, didn't you?' she asked feebly. 'How many parties a night did you cover then?'

'Oh, about five, at the height of the London season . . .' U-M's voice drifted off. 'As I was saying,' she continued, 'my mother had turned the room into a proper nursery, something I never had as a child. The walls were painted pink and there were shelves displaying an assortment of toys and Beatrix Potter bowls, and there were scales for weighing a real baby. A children's playpen stood in the middle of the room and in it, sleeping on a baby's blanket, were five puppies. I remember looking around and thinking my mother should never have had me and that's why my granny brought me up. All along she'd really just wanted to have dogs,' she added cheerfully.

There wasn't a flicker of sympathy or understanding from the journalist, so I moved closer to U-M and licked her hand to show I cared.

'Hello, sweetheart,' she said, looking down at me in surprise. What surprises *me* is she doesn't always realize that I know how she's feeling inside.

'I was finally given a goldfish when I was six,' she continued. 'It wasn't quite what I'd had in mind and one can only spend so much time watching a poor fish swimming around and around in its glass bowl. Sadly, it had suicidal tendencies. Time after time it would throw itself out of the bowl that stood on the grand piano, which was covered by an embroidered Japanese shawl worked in shades of golden silk threads. Unfortunately, the fish blended into the design. Sometimes no one noticed for hours that the bowl was empty. Then I think one day he must have decided that he'd had enough, because he leapt out of the bowl in the middle of the night. By morning he lay still among the golden Japanese lilies. A fitting resting place for a little fish hell-bent on committing hara-kiri.'

There was an awkward silence. Then the journalist spoke. 'Could I have a glass of water, please? Then we'd better get on with the interview.'

I detected a note of desperation in her voice.

U-M sprang up in her high heels, almost sending me flying. 'Of course! Why don't we have something stronger? How about a gin and tonic?'

For the next hour U-M talked animatedly about her career as a society columnist, describing what it was like to be on a round of party-going and how things had changed since 1947 when she'd been a debutante, presented at court to the King and Queen.

I gave her a look of horror. Did she have to advertise how old she was? That's something I thought a lady never did.

She was on a roll now and out came all the old photographs, so I curled up and went to sleep.

What I really wanted to know was did Archie ever get around to giving her a Poodle? What actually happened in 1956?

I Read a Private Letter. Oh Dear!

— In which Toffee chews my Jimmy Choos

I know U-M writes 'spellbinding' novels (according to the
reviewers), but she also seems to be terribly fond of composing
emails, too.

Now I don't like to boast, but my pedigree puts *Debrett's Peerage*
in the shade. I'm sure if I were a human I'd at least be a duchess,
maybe even a princess. So it was a real shock when I read the
following, sent to my breeder just a few weeks after I'd arrived in
London. Was I to be sent back, in disgrace?

Dear Mary,

*When Toffee first arrived she was like a little brown lamb, as good
as gold and quite shy. I have to say that she has now morphed into
a jaw-snapping crocodile of fearsome proportions. Striking with the
lightning speed of a missile, she leaps forward and swings from my
clothes like a bell ringer when I try to get dressed in the morning.
Then she squares her jaw and relentlessly hangs on while her body
sways to and fro in mid-air. Was her mother a trapeze artist? Yesterday*

she seized my right cuff and pulled hard, but it wasn't my cuff she'd got hold of – it was my wrist. It felt like having injections from multiple hypodermic needles and I was left with a line of bleeding pinpricks. I gave a howl of pain and she looked at me as if she thought I was pathetic. 'Low pain threshold, then?' she seemed to say.

Best wishes,
Una-Mary

Well, really, what a fuss! I was just having the time of my life teasing U-M and listening to the satisfying sound of ripping nylons. I emailed Mary myself telling her I was happy, well fed, had been taken for runs in the park and been given a basket of toys, so U-M must quite like me. Mustn't she? I think she'd be lonely if I abandoned her. I even share my huge double bed with her; having turned it down every night myself, I then arrange the soft frilly pillows to my liking so all she has to do is climb in beside me. She can't complain. I even allow her to watch the news headlines on the TV. If people don't approve I tell them that they can catch far worse things from having a man in their bed than they'll ever catch from a dog.

I was very gratified when Mary emailed me back, but she did warn me in the nicest possible way that I had been extremely lucky to be fixed up with a super billet, and I should take care not to push U-M too far.

What am I supposed to do now? Rush out and buy her a bunch of roses? I can't *help* being high-spirited, but I'll have to think of something to please her. Perhaps being obedient for once? No, she might have a heart attack!

Then I had a brainwave. U-M will be so grateful when she finds I've been helping her make the garden look nice. It was jolly hard work but I was sure she'd appreciate my efforts. So, I got a gardening glove out of the tool cupboard and carried it around for a while; but she didn't seem to notice, so I got hold of the empty plastic flower pots that were stacked in a corner, brought them into the house and arranged them in the hall. I was making progress! Next I picked up the dead heads of the roses which she'd left on the ground and carried them one by one into the drawing room, where I arranged them in a pretty pattern on the carpet. What would she do without me? Then I tried really hard to lengthen the hosepipe by pulling it with my teeth so it would reach the flower bed at the bottom of the garden when she next wanted to water it. Suddenly I heard her yell my name. She sounded cross. What had I done now?

'Toffee!' She spoke sternly.

I looked at her with pleading eyes. Honestly, I was only trying to be helpful.

She bent down and stroked my back. 'What are we going to do with you?' she asked despairingly.

Going Barking Mad

Kill it! Kill it! Kill it!

W ould you believe it? Of all the most annoying things
that could happen in the world, this takes the dog biscuit!
I'm furious, not to mention frustrated. I've hardly started
writing my book, and I'm still trying to find out if Archie ever got
around to giving U-M a puppy in 1956, when along comes the
computer man, Mr Expert. In the first place, who asked him to
come and play havoc with our lives? And my career? My book of
observations and my take on life in general is going to make the
bestseller lists, and I'm probably going to end up as the breadwinner
of the family so U-M can put her feet up and drink champagne.
(Not that I will begrudge giving her the odd hand-out.)

To cut a long story short, Mr Expert said we needed a new brain.
Ours was too slow and unreliable. It was, in fact, too old. Speak for
yourself! I need a new brain like I need an agonising migraine! U-M
isn't senile yet so *she* doesn't need a new brain either.

I wanted to get back to work and now I was faced with delays
if we went ahead. If I'd been a nasty little dog I'd have nipped him
on the ankle so he'd have left, never to return. Instead I fished a
toy squirrel out of my basket and shook it to death while Mr Expert
went on insisting that U-M get rid of the tin box on the desk.
What's it ever done to him? I'd never looked upon it as *clever*. For
one thing it lacked common sense; however, it had done as it was
told for nearly seven years so she might have shown it some gratitude. But U-M finally capitulated. Or was she brainwashed?

That's when the nightmare started. A few days later everything
had to stop as the new brain, big and rather flashy, and in fact very
pleased with itself, was installed. Mr Expert beamed at his own
cleverness in unplugging the tired old brain and plugging in this
new wonder box.

'It will be *much* faster than the old one,' he said smugly. I stared
at him, stony-faced. Why should faster always mean better these
days? What's the rush? Will sending an email a nanosecond quicker
change your life? And what are you supposed to do with that extra
second? If U-M is writing a novel, the fastest computer in the world
isn't going to help her work out the twists and turns of the plot,
or choose a character's name or compose a lyrical phrase. This
writing business is about sweat, tears and backache with the occa-
sional flash of inspiration . . . not the speed of a metal container
that resembles a biscuit tin. That box is never in a million years
going to produce *War and Peace* or *Romeo and Juliet* all on its own.
It wasn't long before I heard U-M exclaim in horror.

'Oh, no!' Then she said, 'What's *that*? And how do you . . . ?'
Her voice was filled with mounting panic. She looked Mr Expert
straight in the eye. 'Does this mean that . . . ?'

Yes. It did.

Don't you think Mr Expert might have *warned* us that a new
brain meant a new system? New layouts? We were now going to
have to relearn how everything worked. At high speed, of course!
Don't forget that! We got this new brain at vast expense because it
was so much faster than the old one.

I heard U-M swearing like a trooper. 'I wish I'd kept my old
IBM golf ball typewriter,' she groaned. 'I wrote eleven books on it
and it was so *easy.*'

At that point I thought it better not to point out that a computer
might be just a teensy-weensy bit quicker . . .

The Facts of Life

Where *is* my ball?

A t last! I found a photograph of U-M's son and daughter, with . . . wait for it . . . a cream Poodle with long, silky, pale amber-coloured ears. On the back she'd written *Baba and Buffy with Amber, Cornwall, 1958.*

So Archie had kept his promise! Amber looked about two and I had to quell a pang of jealousy because she was awfully pretty, with big dark eyes and a sweet face. It so happened that U-M had her eldest granddaughter, Sophie, to tea that afternoon.

I positioned myself in a nearby chair so I could hear what they were saying.

'Was that your first dog?' Sophie asked, glancing at the picture that was propped up on a side table. 'Have you always had Poodles?'

I perked up my ears. This was going to be interesting.

'Yes, always. For one thing they don't moult, so asthmatics don't react to them. They're also one of the most intelligent breed of dogs in the world. In the old days they used to perform and do tricks in circuses.'

I stood up and raised my head, stretching my elegant neck, and preened. She was right. We are a brilliant breed.

'Which is the cleverest breed, then?'

'The Border Collie,' U-M replied instantly. 'It's amazing how they herd sheep.'

I kept quiet. I've a story to tell you about that in due course but right now I wanted to hear more about Amber.

'How long did you have Amber for?' Sophie asked.

'Nearly seventeen years. They're among the longest-living dogs. I know someone whose Poodle is nineteen.'

Sophie nodded in understanding. 'Truffle's death was shocking, wasn't it? How old was she?'

'Only four and a half. That was dreadful.' Her voice was subdued and she looked sad.

Who was Truffle? Why had nobody told me about her?

'Amber was very sporty,' U-M continued, brightening again. 'She adored being on the beach in Cornwall and when we went to Scotland she'd climb the hills like a mountain goat. The idea that Poodles are silly little lap dogs with ribbons in their hair is so outdated.'

Hear, hear! I couldn't agree more.

U-M poured Sophie another cup of tea and I just knew U-M was on a roll. I'd better sit down again and see if I could pick up any more information.

'She had twins,' U-M announced.

What was that? Had I heard right?

'Did you help deliver them?' Sophie asked.

'No. She had to have a caesarean.'

This was interesting. A Poodle that was too posh to push.

'As there were only two puppies,' U-M continued, 'they were too big for her to give birth by herself. The vet picked her up and took her back to the surgery. It was such a relief when they phoned me later to say she was fine and she'd had a boy and a girl.

'That evening the couple who owned Socrates, the silver Poodle who had 'married' Amber, according to the children, came to see his offspring.' U-M was laughing at the memory. 'He wasn't that interested in the puppies but he was all over Amber. I think he was recalling how much he'd enjoyed himself the last time they'd met.' That was too much information for me! I hopped down and strolled into the garden. I'm really glad I've been spared s-e-x for medical reasons. Mary Brotherton had told U-M I was too young at the time and I'd never mature; I'd always be like a puppy. 'I don't mind,' she'd replied loyally. Now, of course, she boasts that I'm still like a puppy. When a male dog persistently jumped on me last summer at the beach, I'd been so angry I finally snapped at him. How dare he molest me? U-M had finally gone over to his owner and asked politely if he'd keep his dog on a lead as I'd been spayed and didn't like what he was doing.

The young man had apologised. 'Sorry about that,' he'd explained. 'The thing is my dog's had the snip too, but I'm sure he remembers what it was like before and hopes that if he keeps trying, everything will come back!'

When I Was Badly Attacked

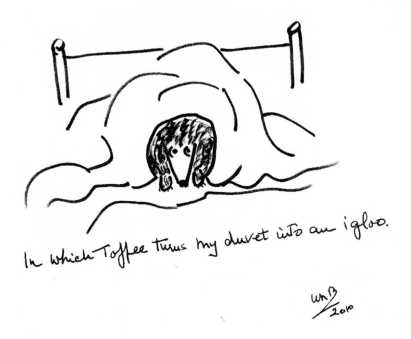

In which Toffee turns my duvet into an igloo.

WnB/2010

I'd have been no more than four months old when U-M was asked if she could put up a friend of a friend when he stayed in London. He travelled a lot so it would only be for a couple of nights every month or so and, hospitable as ever, she said yes. That was her first mistake.

He seemed a nice enough chap, polite and undemanding, giving me a pat and saying he missed his two dogs back home. We hardly saw him when he did come to stay so we jogged along happily for a time. Little did we know how it would all end.

One Saturday morning when he was staying U-M had to go out for an hour to do some shopping. As I was still a baby she shut me in her room with my toys and a bowl of water so I'd be snug and safe and not get into any mischief. Her words, not mine!

Suddenly the bedroom door opened and the man came bounding into the room. I can barely remember what happened next because I was so frightened – blows rained down on me like hammers and I was kicked viciously across the floor. I know I tried to dodge his fists and feet but I was in such pain I could hardly move and I felt sick. Then he slammed out of the room, banging the door behind him. A few minutes later I heard the crash of the front door as he went out.

Why did he attack me? I'd only been barking at a passing van. I curled up and waited for U–M to return.

U–M came back minutes later, smiling and saying, 'Hello, Toffee! Have you been a good girl, darling?'

I was so pleased to see her I wanted to run towards her, but I couldn't. There was something wrong with my back legs. I couldn't walk so, using my front paws, I tried to drag myself forward.

'What's the matter?' she asked, scooping me up with her hands because I was still very small.

I remember screaming with pain so she quickly put me down. She looked stricken. 'Oh, my God! What's happened?'

Then she phoned Kevin Clifford at the Brompton Veterinary Clinic and explained she'd found me in great pain but had no idea how it could have happened.

If only I could have told her. If only there'd been someone else in the house who could have told her.

The next thing I knew, U–M had wrapped me up in a soft blanket and was carrying me carefully in her arms as we went in search of a taxi.

'Wot's 'appened to the little feller?' the taxi driver asked as we settled in the back of his cab.

'I wish I knew,' U–M replied in a shaky voice.

Mr Clifford asked the same question as he examined me. I shivered although I wasn't really cold. 'Has something heavy fallen on her like a table or a bookcase?' he asked.

'There's nothing in my bedroom that can fall over. All the cupboards are built in and, apart from the bed, there's just a big armchair and the television on a low table. What I don't understand is the room was exactly as I'd left it when I got back. The only explanation I can think of is she might have tried to jump up on to the bed, which is quite high, and then fallen off it backwards, landing on her bottom.'

He looked doubtful. 'I'm going to keep her in for observation and we'll X-ray her. I'll ring you later on today to let you know how she is.'

U-M nodded, shocked.

I don't remember much about the rest of the day and I must have nodded off when they X-rayed me. It was much later in the afternoon when U-M came to collect me and she looked very concerned. They'd told her on the phone what they'd discovered but she could hardly take it in.

'How can Toffee's pelvis be fractured in five places?' she kept saying. 'How the hell could that have happened?'

Mr Clifford shook his head, equally puzzled. Then I heard him tell her what was to happen.

'Toffee must be immobilized for eight weeks in a small cage,' he advised. 'You can lift her out carefully several times a day and carry her into your garden and place her gently on the ground to do her business, but don't let her walk at all. Keep her in a small warm room on her own, and keep the curtains drawn all the time. She'll think it's night and that will encourage her to sleep. Don't let her get excited. She must be kept quiet and let her have a bowl of water in the cage. I've given her a pain-killing injection which should see her through the night,' he added 'but if you have any problems just give us a ring.'

'Thank you.' U-M sounded profoundly grateful and relieved that at least I wasn't about to kick the bucket.

'Bring her back in eight weeks and we'll X-ray her again to make sure her pelvis has healed.'

If U-M's brain was having a problem grappling with all this, my mind was on a rollercoaster. In one fell swoop I'd heard I was to be imprisoned for two months, but at least I was going home, even if I was going to have to sleep alone for the first time in my whole life.

You'd think that was the end of the story, wouldn't you? I made a full recovery thanks to U-M, who did a very good impersonation of Florence Nightingale by feeding me exquisite morsels of chicken, with steamed carrots and broccoli. But it wasn't.

A year later, when U-M was out shopping once again on Saturday morning, it happened again. And this time the man tried to strangle me with my collar, and very nearly succeeded. I was fully grown by then and managed to put up a fight.

But how was U-M to know the man was an evil maniac? He'd been so sympathetic when I'd 'mysteriously' broken my pelvis and agreed with U-M that I must have fallen off her bed.

When U-M found me shivering in her room, she knew something had happened again.

'What on earth is going on?' she exclaimed, glancing around the tidy room. She stroked my back. I winced; he'd hit me with his fist, bruising me. Something then made her reach for my collar. I always keep it on, night and day.

'Oh my God!' Instinctively she rushed down to the kitchen. How did she know she'd find the evidence there? I refused to follow her. It was too soon. After he'd punched me and I'd run out of the bedroom to try and escape he'd come after me, and that was when he cornered me in the kitchen by grabbing my leather collar and twisting it until the leather broke. It had been a fight to the death. Wouldn't you think he'd have hidden the evidence? U-M apparently went straight to the dustbin by the hob and opened it. There the savagely broken pale blue collar lay on top of the rubbish.

Hell hath no fury like a dog owner when her animal has been viciously assaulted. She told him to get out of the house *now*. It was obvious he'd broken my pelvis the previous year. Now he'd tried to strangle me. She phoned the RSPCA.

He denied everything. Although he was still in his pyjamas he declared he'd been out all morning. He even went so far as to ask her sweetly if she'd like him to take me to the vet!

'I love dogs!' he kept insisting.

Then she kicked him out of the house and had the front door locks changed. After he'd gone, she discovered he'd left a lot of stuff in his room, so with the help of her son, Buffy, it was taken to a friend's warehouse, and Buffy left a message on his voicemail to tell him where he could retrieve his belongings.

Drama was to turn into sheer farce. This man left two messages on Buffy's voicemail that night. Both were death threats for U-M, so now we had the police as well as the RSPCA involved. He denied everything but let slip to someone else that my barking had 'annoyed' him.

It left me wondering what he would do if he got *really* angry.

A Weekend in the Country and a Sad Loss

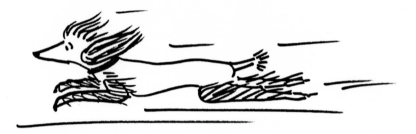

Toffee auditioning for the Grand National

T alking of being versatile and able to turn my paw to anything, I did a spot of sheepherding up in Herefordshire a while ago. The sheep were most obedient, getting in a cluster and trotting like mad as I ran around them in circles. I didn't know why they made such a strange bleating noise, so I barked more loudly to encourage them to talk properly.

I was so disappointed when U-M's hostess started yelling angrily at me.

'Toffee!' she screamed. 'Here! Bad girl! Heel!' Then she looked at U-M reproachfully. 'Dogs get shot for doing that,' she snapped.

Well, how was I supposed to know they weren't cousins of mine? Their coats were woolly like mine and I wasn't hurting them. They were the size of Standard Poodles, too. Not so graceful, though. Perhaps they thought one of them had given birth to a brown lamb instead of a black sheep? We were just having a lovely game of chase and I certainly brightened up their day. Poor things, stuck in a field with no one to talk to.

'They do have similar coats,' U-M remarked mildly as she slipped one of my favourite biscuits into my mouth to comfort me. I'm not used to being scolded; taking everything into consideration, I'm a good girl. Most of the time, anyway. Our walk continued in silence as I trotted obediently by U-M's side, but I could sense the heavy cloud of disapproval hanging over me and I don't think we'll be staying with that friend again.

U-M has her faults, like leaving me at home while she goes to the theatre or out to a dinner party, but she is enormously loyal. It's a case of love-me-love-my-dog, and woe betide anyone who isn't nice to me.

We often spend the weekend on the Isle of Wight, staying with Baba and her husband Rob, and that's really fun. They have a Norfolk Terrier, Millie, who is my best friend. Millie and I like to gallop shoulder to shoulder around the land and forest that surrounds the house. I even get to sleep on a grand antique four-poster bed!

The most important thing I've learnt is to write thank you letters when we return home. Sometimes I send a photograph of myself which can be displayed – framed, I should think – on the recipient's mantelpiece, or else I send one of U-M's drawings of me. I have to make sure she's signed it, too. Who knows? A portrait of me could be really valuable one day; and I don't mean a photocopy!

Talking about photographs, I noticed a picture of a beautiful-looking Poodle in U-M's Filofax the other day, and with a shock I realized it wasn't me! What's going on? Buffy's children, Lucy, Amelia, Archie, Charlotte and Edward had come to lunch and U-M was looking up a phone number when this picture fell out.

'Oh, that's Truffle,' she exclaimed, holding it up so everyone could see it. I jumped on her lap, almost shouting *What about me?* I'd temporarily forgotten hearing Truffle being mentioned before. Such a nice name, too. It is an ongoing embarrassment that U-M picked my name from a menu, apparently whilst saying, 'I love sticky toffee pudding. It would be a good name for a brown dog, wouldn't it?'

No. I don't think so. When she's in a good mood she calls me (wait for it!) 'Pud-Pud'. In the park when I'm cantering around and she wants me to go back to her, she calls 'Pud-Pud' as loudly as she can. Then she praises me for being so obedient, but in reality I'm merely tearing back to shut her up.

'Good Puddy,' she'll then croon. Oh, God! Why didn't she call me something like Shadow, or Lulu after my mother?

U-M seems to enjoy humiliating me. When it's dark, she insists on attaching a blazing light to my collar so that I'm flashing like an ambulance, visible for miles around.

Archie broke into my thoughts by asking, 'What exactly happened to Truffle?'

There was a pause, and I knew U-M didn't want to upset her young grandchildren.

'Truffle became very ill and she had to be put to sleep,' U-M said carefully, though there was pain in her voice. Archie nodded in silent understanding.

'Would anyone like some chocolate cake?' U-M asked brightly. I still don't know how Truffle died, and maybe I never will.

Animals Galore

Want to play?

unp./2010

It struck me the other day that U-M being deprived of having a pet when she was a child would account for her going completely overboard when Baba and Buffy were small, ending up with seventeen pets in a comparatively small London house with just a little paved garden at the back. This would have been between the Sixties and Seventies, when you could still park your car round the corner outside Harrods night and day, which they apparently did. Listening to her talk to Jessica, her granddaughter, as they sat having lunch in the garden, I also learned that the milk was delivered every morning in a horse-drawn cart and U-M put on a smart hat and gloves even to go out to buy a pound of potatoes. The television picture was only black and white in those days, and there was one telephone in each house that most people had on a table in the hall. It all sounds very nice and peaceful and Amber must have enjoyed the simple life of those days.

I have to cope with everything from emails to Twitter and I *hate* mobile phones. Why does everyone have to snatch them the second they ring as if they were unexploded bombs? Something must be very important indeed to justify halting a private conversation between friends. Or is it that there's someone *more* important to talk to? Let the damn thing ring! Or better still, switch it off. You're unlikely to miss a call of earth-shattering significance.

So there was U-M and Archie with their two children and Amber, living a peaceful and tranquil life when *wham!* U-M gets two cats, one of which was an abandoned kitten she found in the front area of a nearby deserted house. This was followed by Floppy Hanse, a white house-trained Angora rabbit who used to sit on her knee in the evening and watch television. By this time I would imagine Amber must have been having an identity crisis: was she their third baby or a cat? The cats must have wondered if they were dogs, or whether they might possibly be rabbits? I once heard U-M say they all copied each other, so the cats were growling and Amber was opening doors with a hooked paw and Floppy Hanse was digging a burrow in the garden as if she was heading for Australia. When asked if squabbling ever broke out between them all, she replied blithely, 'No, never. As long as the newcomer was very young, the older animals rally around to look after it.'

That wasn't the end. Next came three terrapins in a tank with little rocks for them to climb over, followed by six goldfish in another tank and four budgerigars in a huge cage. At one point there was even a real little duckling paddling away in the bath. Buffy had found it looking lost in Hyde Park's Serpentine and had decided to 'rescue' it. At first U-M was enchanted – 'I could tell everyone I had a real duck in my bath' – but then she decided it would be kinder to return it to the park where she was sure he'd find his real mother.

However when Buffy, who had caught on to the 'let's-start-a-zoo' craze, stepped over the mark, the word 'no' was heard for the first time. He came home from school one afternoon and proudly produced a small white rat from his blazer pocket.

The first thing U-M said was, 'For goodness' sake, don't let the cats see it because they'll kill it.' This would have been difficult because it was peeping over Buffy's open shirt collar by then. The second thing she said was, 'I'm afraid you'll have to take it back to wherever you got it because it will attract all the other rats in the area and the house will become infested.'

It sounds to me as if the house was already 'infested' with several different species of God's creatures, so would one more have made any difference?

I'm thankful there's only U-M and me on our own these days. How could she be my full-time companion if there were lots of other animals around? I'd hate the rivalry too. Supposing she liked a cat more than me? Of course, it's unthinkable. How could she possibly like anyone more than me?

My Fans Spoil Me

Toffee always finds the best place to sleep.

I got an email today from Mary Brotherton. It began, 'Happy Birthday, Darling Toffee.' I had sent her a gentle reminder early that morning that said:

Happy Birthday to me. Happy Birthday to me. Happy Birthday to adorable, sweet and beautiful Toffee on her birthday. Happy Birthday to me!

I'm glad she got the message. She went on to say:

Many thanks for your letter and I hope you have a very happy birthday and many more to come. Take care – you don't realize how very lucky you are to have found U-M so take care of her, too. All your friends here send you their love. Mary.

I love keeping in touch with all my fans, and I treasure all their presents. U-M's housekeeper, Maria, who helps look after us, is always giving me lovely presents, including a furry little fox cub that squeaks, a life-size rubber chicken, a bouncy ball and a large, soft, dark brown fake fur rug. There's only one problem: when I go to sleep on it I vanish into its dark fluffiness as my coat is exactly the same colour.

'Toffee?' U-M calls anxiously. 'Where are you?' She doesn't trust me, and this is because I've been known to sneak off and scout around the house, helping myself to make-up brushes, pens and pencils, reading glasses and money if I can get hold of it. Especially fifty pound notes, because they're such a pretty colour. So I raise my head from the fur rug and look at her, thinking, is there no rest for the wicked? Can't I even have forty winks without her thinking I'm up to mischief?

'Oh! You're *there!*' she exclaims in surprise. I stretch my legs. I think it's time I took her for a long, brisk walk. She was cross with me yesterday for all of two minutes because I'd grabbed a letter she'd received that morning from her accountant, and then I'd galloped to the top of the house. By the time she'd caught up with me I'd turned it into such pretty confetti. Didn't she realize I'd done her a favour? She hates dealing with her accounts and this way I've saved her the bother. I must do it more often in future. If I was a secretary, think how much time and hassle I'd save my employer!

When I was younger I fancied pretty jewellery. That had to stop after an incident when we were staying on the Isle of Wight.

One morning Baba went up to U-M, who was standing by the open front door. She held out her hand to show U-M a pair of diamond stud earrings.

'They're beautiful,' U-M observed, impressed.

'Rob gave them to me for my birthday,' her daughter remarked rather pointedly.

At that point I decided to go for a little walk in the garden.

I heard Baba say, 'I left them on my bedside table before I went to sleep last night and I've just found them scattered on the doormat.'

That was when I thought I'd better inspect the tennis court as well as the garden. Perhaps U-M should give Baba a jewellery box for her next birthday?

The Pros and Cons

Truffle having a monumental Sulk.

umb
2010

To have or not to have? That is the *real* life-changing question. I hear so many people talking to U-M about wanting a dog but at the same time putting forward reasons why they can't have one. A dog really isn't a Christmas present you can dump on a cold rainy day in January, nor is it a toy you can play with when you're in the mood but stuff back in a cupboard when you have better things to do.

Dogs have rights as well as humans, and they have no way of protesting to the police that they've been abandoned miles from home on a motorway, or starved and beaten.

There's a saying: 'If you want one year's happiness have an affair, and if you want years and years of happiness get a dog.'

Here are the choices that face human beings:

Pros of having a dog:	Pros of *not* having a dog:
Receiving a big welcome when you return home.	You can put things on the floor and no one will touch them.
You can stagger home late and you won't be nagged.	Your shoes won't get chewed.
You never have to sleep alone.	You needn't go out if it's raining.
Waking up knowing you can make your dog happy.	You can sleep until noon if you want to.
You have a reason to go for a walk and get some fresh air.	You can have a leisurely breakfast and read the newspapers.
You are provided with amusement, laughter and company.	Every room in the house smells fresh.
Enjoying the reflected glory of having a beautiful dog.	You won't tread on anything nasty in the garden.
Making new friends; at least your dog will. Why not go along for the ride?	Eating in peace with no one demanding scraps from your plate.
Provides an excuse for refusing unwanted invitations.	No one will dangle from your dressing-gown cord.
Forgetting your companion is a dog ('Look at those lovely daffodils, Toffee!')	
Someone who doesn't get jealous, asking who you're talking to on the phone.	
Someone who doesn't dislike what you're wearing just as you're leaving to go to a party.	

Here we are at the end and I was afraid I didn't have enough points in favour!

There you have it. Take your pick. And what is it about having a human companion that we dogs like?

I have to be absolutely honest and say the most important thing for us is to be fed regularly with good food suited to our digestion. No scraps from people's plates, no fatty foods and certainly no chocolate in any form. Why are certain dog shops selling chocolate eclairs, meringues and fairy cakes 'specially made for dogs'? How can they be? If they don't contain butter, cream, chocolate and flour what are they made of? I think I must write to the Prime Minister and get him to pass a bill that makes it an offence to sell or give dogs what you might be tempted to give children; although it's probably bad for them too.

We also like bowls of fresh water every day. Regular walks, long or short, are vital, and good for humans, too. And finally, a comfortable bed.

That's about it, really. We're not demanding and we don't throw a wobbly if we're denied the latest iPods, computers and fancy trainers. We love companionship, being patted and stroked, and most of all we like routine, being taught no means *no*, and given boundaries which we mustn't cross. Myself? I'm not adverse to a bit of spoiling now and again. Only as a special treat, of course! (I hope U-M takes the hint.)

Take my word for it. You'll never find a truer friend than a dog.

How I Became a Celebrity

Toffee, aged Twelve Weeks, Steals a Smoked Salmon blini.

I don't like to boast but I have to admit I am a bit of a celebrity. In Richard Kay's column in the *Daily Mail* I was described as 'Toffee, who rarely has a dull moment'. This was when U-M broke her hip and I climbed on her chest to see if she was still alive, a gesture I don't think she fully appreciated at the time. This happened nine days before we were due to stay with Millie on the Isle of Wight. I went ahead to be with them and was looked after by Baba, and U-M managed to make it on Christmas Eve, with the help of Buffy who drove her down. Afterwards she said it was the best Christmas she'd ever had. That I think was due to the bottle of morphine the hospital gave her, laced, as you do, with champagne!

On another occasion *The Mail on Sunday* showed a very nice photograph of me sitting on U-M's lap. I'm looking very cool and collected and really rather pretty. Sadly I can't say the same about her, but she had been put through a bit of an ordeal.

The previous evening we'd made the mistake of going out for our last walk at ten o'clock, which we did every night. It was a balmy September evening and the moon shone down on us, rivalling the brightness of the streetlamps. A gentle breeze ruffled my coat and U-M and I were in a very happy mood. Fifteen minutes later we arrived home again, climbing the front steps and unlocking the door. Once in the hall she turned to shut it, but there was a loud thump and the door wouldn't shut because a masked man with a baseball cap pulled well down was pushing his way into the house. He shoved U-M roughly up against the wall and started beating her up. I must say she put up a fight, hitting him back and yelling 'Get out! Get out!' But then he slammed his white cotton glove over her mouth and at that moment a second man bounded into the hall, also masked, gloved and wearing a cap.

I'm told I did the sensible thing by remaining silent, although I do bark like mad at everyone else when they arrive, be they friend or foe. Instinct told me these two robbers meant business. The police said they'd have killed me with one blow to the head if I'd made a noise to attract attention. They'd silenced U-M but her eyes were blazing with anger.

'We want your jewellery,' the first man said as he ripped the rings off her left hand. Then he dragged her up the stairs to the bedroom. The other man grabbed my lead and, tying me to the banister rail in the hall, went upstairs also.

'Where's your jewellery?' the first one was still shouting.

'In the drawer over there,' U-M replied, icily calm. I could hear the second man ransacking the other rooms. This went on for a while and I wondered what was going to happen next.

'Where's the safe?' I heard one of them ask.

'I don't have a safe,' U-M replied calmly. This was true. We've never had a safe. He didn't believe her.

'I know you've got a safe. We've been told you have a safe. Someone has seen it. Come on, where is it?' This was a nasty moment. If they didn't believe her, what would they do? Torture her until they got it out of her? Pull the whole house apart?

'I do not have a safe and I have never had a safe,' I heard her retort imperiously. Straining to hear what was happening, I was rather surprised by his next question.

'Have you got a plastic bag I could put everything in?' It was like a comedy sketch when the bank robbers threaten the staff and then produce water pistols.

'Will this Harrods bag do?' U-M asked. I detected a flicker of sarcasm in her voice. I didn't hear the answer and then I heard her speak again and this time I realized she was at breaking point.

'Can I go downstairs to make sure my dog's alright?'

'No. Your dog is fine,' he snapped sharply.

'But I'm very worried about her.' She spoke with desperation now. 'I just want to make sure—'

'Sit on the bed and shut up.' Then there was an explosion of bad words and then silence. If she was worried about me then I was even more worried about her.

Amazingly they left a few minutes later, but one of them swore at me and tried to kick me as he headed for the front door. Then they were gone with their haul. Never before has a Harrods plastic carrier bag been so heavily laden with beautiful jewellery and a cash box they'd found containing over a hundred pounds.

U-M came flying down the stairs and when she saw me practically dangling from the banister, she bent down to unclip my lead, saying, 'Oh, Toffee. Are you all right, darling? You poor little girl.' Then she picked me up and hugged me. I don't know if they meant to hang me but if I hadn't kept calm and been very still they'd have succeeded.

She phoned the police and then Baba, who insisted on coming round with her husband, Rob. Then U-M phoned Buffy, who was away for the weekend and who also wanted to drive up to London to be with us, but she wouldn't let him.

It was eleven o'clock at night by now, and within minutes the house was swarming with nice policemen and women and a lady who was dressed like an astronaut but was apparently 'from forensics'.

It was a long night. Baba kept everyone going with cups of tea and then a policewoman asked U-M to take off the beautiful black-and-white silk dress she was wearing so it could be examined for DNA.

'You could put on an old pair of jeans and a casual top instead,' she assured U-M kindly.

One of the policemen raised his eyebrows and observed, 'I very much doubt if this lady has a pair of jeans or anything casual either,' he observed with amusement.

He was right. She may have been roughly manhandled and had all of her jewellery stolen, but she came sailing back a few minutes later wearing a very smart red dress.

A week later I thought I was heading for real stardom. First, oh, the excitement! Then, oh, the disappointment!

I thought my Big Moment had arrived. Lights! Camera! Action! I was about to pose, ready for my close-up, eyes wide and my chin up because, as we came out of our house, a camera crew was setting up their equipment on the pavement.

U-M looked puzzled. She's used to being photographed, but they weren't setting up for her either.

Then we saw a model being helped into a coat, an assistant holding her hat while a make-up artist added more blusher to her pale cheeks.

'Let's move higher up the street – the light is better there,' the photographer said, and they trailed off behind him.

I watched them leave with a sinking heart. It struck me; might I have had my fifteen minutes of fame already? I do hope not. I do so want to be famous. This was a crushing blow to my self-esteem. My coat was much better than the model's, too.

All I could do was console myself with the thought that for supper I was having chicken and rice, with freshly steamed carrots and broccoli, cooked specially for me by our housekeeper, Maria. Her Majesty's dogs may eat out of silver bowls, but I bet they don't have their very own chef.

'Did you want your picture taken, Toffee?' Maria asked, whipping out her mobile. I posed at once, sitting very regally and looking straight into the lens. There was a click.

'Look!' Maria said triumphantly. U-M looked at the bright little screen.

'That's very good,' she said. 'Could you get a printout of it for me?'

So the day didn't end so badly after all. Maybe I will be really famous one day.

I'd Hang Them!

— (4 Which Toffee doesn't want to go that way!

'That's 'terrible!' I heard U-M exclaim in a shocked voice. I pricked up my ears. She usually says, 'No! I don't believe it!' when she reads about a scandal that is, I think, highly believable. We all know that professional footballers earn ridiculous amounts of money. Grown men playing with a ball? I do it in the garden every day and nobody pays me anything. I could do with a few bob! Vet fees can be expensive, what with regular injections and care. Thank goodness for the RSPCA. Everyone should be made to donate money to them every year for the wonderful work they do.

I'm one of the lucky dogs to go to a good home. Mary Brotherton, who bred me, checked U-M to make sure I'd be properly looked after. Wicked breeders don't care as long as they make lots of money. I have to say that for all her faults U-M would go hungry rather than let me starve.

Here's an idea! Why don't they make footballers give a million pounds for every match they play to the RSPCA!

It might mean the WAGS would be deprived of masses of short, tight-fitting clothes, hair dye, false eyelashes and, of course, acrylic nails, but what a brilliant way to keep some of us who are not as lucky as me happy and healthy.

'This is really dreadful; I had no idea,' U-M says angrily as she gazes at the newspaper. Is there a government scandal? Has another newspaper been caught tapping the Queen's private telephone? I go over to where she's sitting on the sofa.

I spot a big photograph of a sad-looking Spaniel.

'Have you read this?' she asks her son Buffy as he comes into the room.

Without waiting for an answer, she continues, 'Did you know that people who steal a dog, or cat, or any sort of pet, only get a caution and a fine? That's no more than what they'd get if they stole your mobile or your laptop, both of which can be replaced in five minutes,' she adds acidly. She sounded very angry, and so she should. Bring back hanging, I say! It's utterly cruel to both the humans and their pets.

The owners are left desperately upset and frantically worried. It's the not knowing what has happened to their pet that's the worst part. I think U-M would be distraught if I vanished on a walk, never perhaps to be seen again. For someone like me it's terrifying to even think of being bundled away by strangers to a place that's unfamiliar. Will they feed me? Dogs are 100 per cent dependent on humans when it comes to food, while cats can kill their prey and eat it, and rabbits and horses can eat grass. Then there's the bond with human companions that is so binding. The very routine of the day is vital to our happiness. I don't know what I'd do if someone dognapped me.

Some members of Parliament want those who steal pets to serve a prison sentence of up to seven years. Hear, hear!

U-M spoke again. 'Did you know that a hundred *thousand* pets were stolen last year?' I jumped on to the sofa and sat close to her, just to remind her I was still around.

'It says here,' she continued, 'that they are warning people not to be taken in by strangers who have a beautiful little dog on a lead. They say their mother has died and they can't look after her dog because they have to go to work. Then they say the dog is for sale for £700 or whatever. Quite a few parents with children who feel sorry for the dog buy it on the spot.'

I don't like the sound of this at all.

'There's a happy ending to one story,' she said brightly. 'A family whose dog had been stolen saw it being walked by another family who admitted they'd been conned into buying it, so the dog was returned to its rightful owners. Other dogs who've been stolen get sent to Ireland or Wales for breeding purposes. In due course their puppies are born, returned to England with fake Kennel Club pedigrees and sold for vast amounts to pet shops.'

I feel like howling. It takes so little to love a dog and provide a happy home. I'm scared now, really frightened. I give a little whimper. A nice dog biscuit would cheer me up no end!

Then U-M starts reading again. 'The most popular dogs that get stolen are Labradors, Springer and Cocker Spaniels and 'handbag' dogs like Pugs!'

What? Not Poodles, which are now recognized as among the most intelligent breeds of dog? Not to mention the prettiest, best behaved, longest living and best companion anyone could ever have! I'm quite upset now that I'm not popular enough to steal. I look at U-M sadly. I feel like a reject.

'Do you want a biscuit, my darling?' she asks me. Not Buffy. *Me.* My wistful expression works every time. She gets up and goes to the cupboard where they are kept and I wag my tail. A nice little biscuit has given me the courage to listen as U-M continues to read the article.

'Over a thousand dogs were stolen last year but in spite of the police's efforts, only ninety-eight arrests were made. That's a disgrace.' To be stolen would mean no treats. Just people who wanted to make money. The very thought was making me feel sick and I jumped up on U-M's lap to reassure myself it would never happen to me.

I remember hearing what U-M had suffered when Kitty vanished many years ago. Kitty was a very beautiful long-haired cat with tortoiseshell markings. I've seen many photographs of her.

I remember U-M telling her grandson, Edward, all about her. Kitty loved our garden and the adjacent gardens – she'd jump down to the pavement, walk round to the front of our house and sit on the window sill, waiting to be let in. It happened every day and as she never crossed the road U-M and her husband, Archie, were quite happy to let her enjoy her freedom. Apparently a well-dressed man came to the door and showed U-M a snapshot. It was a picture of Kitty on someone's big balcony tucking into a bowl of salmon. Then the man started ticking U-M off for letting her cat run around freely.

'I stopped one day and she jumped into my car and I took her home with me,' he said blandly. U-M was appalled and told him in no uncertain words that he had no right to take her cat home. Kitty was hers and it would be very unfair to keep her permanently indoors. The man left and life continued happily. Then one day Kitty vanished. U-M was frantic, putting pictures of Kitty on railings and lampposts in our area. I heard her tell Edward that the worst part was never knowing what had happened to her.

Then a road sweeper told her he'd found a tabby cat that had been run over. She went at once to see the body but it wasn't Kitty. Then it dawned on U-M that this horrible man had most likely catnapped her. She didn't know his name or where he lived.

That's why this newspaper article had touched a raw nerve.

'People who steal animals deserve to be severely punished.' I heard her say to Buffy.

In my opinion they should be hanged!

The Beauty Parlour

Tollee — AKA 'Fraggle Rock'

D ogs that moult all the time are a damned nuisance. You
go into their home and there are drifts of hair in every
corner. The sofa's covered with them, so when a person
stands up they look as if they've spent the night on the floor of a
barber's shop. You can't brush them off either. You have to buy
what looks like a small rolling pin that's covered with a sticky
surface and you roll it all over your clothes. It finally does the trick
but what do you then do with a rolling pin that has sprouted a
wig?

Why not save yourself all that hassle and get a dog that doesn't
moult in the first place? I'm referring to the Poodle or the Bichon
Frisé.

We have wool like a lamb and I've heard of a lady who keeps

her Poodle's clippings, then spins the wool into strands and knits a scarf. Nothing is softer and warmer than Poodle wool. I might set up a business one day of products made from our coats. I would market it as a *Poolmina*. Better than a Pashmina any day!

I like to be clipped every two months, otherwise I resemble a character from *Fraggle Rock* and I can't see where I'm going because my fringe grows too long.

When I arrived in London from Shropshire I realized I'd have to look glamorous; and I *don't* mean wearing diamante collars, ribbons tying my hair back and my long nails painted scarlet. I may have been named after something on a dessert menu but I'm *not* a tart! I feel so sorry for dogs who are humanized with fancy clothes. For goodness' sake, have a baby if you want to dress something up! Some people have the nerve to dye our coats; U-M once saw a woman in a rose-pink dress who'd had her white Poodle dyed pink to match! It's these vain and stupid women who have given us a bad name. Men especially think we're namby-pamby silly little things, which only a silly little woman would want.

We are as much of a sporty country dog as any Labrador and we were originally bred to retrieve ducks from freezing water, thus the pompoms of wool were to protect our knee and ankle joints. We are not pretty little spoilt dogs who will sit primly on a silk cushion, but courageous and clever companions – as U-M will firmly tell people who smirk and say with obvious amusement, 'Oh, you've got a Poodle!'

U-M loved my coat when I was small. Poodle puppies have long, silky hair and it's not curly at all. She took me to a beauty parlour for dogs and I had a lovely bath and blow dry. She couldn't stop stroking me while exclaiming, 'Oh Toffee! Your coat is so soft and it feels like silk.'

Everyone admired me for my beauty. When the time came to have another wash and blow-dry she took me back to the same place, but tragically it was a different girl this time. U-M told her not to cut my hair because it didn't need it. 'Will you freshen her up with a bath and a blow-dry? Nothing else.' U-M said.

The girl nodded, telling U-M to come and collect me in two hours' time. Then I was whisked away. When U-M returned she cut me dead and then asked the girl if I was ready to come home.

The girl giggled. Why do stupid girls always giggle? 'This *is* Toffee,' she smirked, pointing to me. U-M looked appalled. 'But I told you she was only to be washed and dried. I didn't want her to be clipped.'

She giggled again. 'Her coat was matted at the roots but it will soon grow again.'

I thought U-M was about to explode. 'But it won't be straight and silky again. The truth is you were lazy and couldn't be bothered to brush her coat before you bathed her like the other girl did.'

At that moment I caught sight of my reflection and was devastated to see what had happened. I'd been shaved from top to toe. Even my beautiful ears were naked little skinny flaps. I'd swept into that salon like a prize-winning, highly bred Poodle. Now I was leaving looking like a Mongrel Whippet. There was no way anyone could say I looked even remotely nice.

As we walked home in silence a passing man remarked, 'Short haircut, eh?'

What if U-M no longer wanted to keep me? I looked at her sadly, hoping she still loved me . . . at that moment she picked me up and gave me a cuddle.

'Poor Toffee,' she said comfortingly. 'We certainly won't go there again.' In the Fifties she always had someone come to the house to wash, trim and clip her other Poodle, Amber.

'If I can find someone who will come to us it will be nice for Toffee,' she said. 'Dogs are always happier in their own home.'

Maybe not always. Jane seemed like a nice girl when she arrived with her equipment, and the only thing she requested was a radio playing loud music.

'It keeps dogs happy and then they stand still while being clipped,' she explained.

U-M smiled with amusement and produced a radio, telling the girl she wanted me to have a lamb cut, which means no pompoms. Then she left us in order to work on her next book.

Quite frankly, the girl was hopeless. She tugged at my woolly coat, pulled it and hurt me when she nipped me with her clippers. I shouted at her. I yelled blue murder when she tried to shave my face in a rough way. At one point I thought she was going to blind me. Now I knew why she wanted a radio playing loudly. She'd hoped U-M wouldn't hear my shrieks as I was tortured!

U-M came hurtling into the room, demanding to know what was wrong.

Jane burst into tears. U-M looked around at the scattered tufts of my coat all over the floor. The girl sobbed, 'Toffee is such a *bully!*'

Moi? I'm as gentle as a new-born lamb and I was only a year old at the time.

'That's ridiculous,' U-M protested. 'You obviously don't know how to handle a dog and look at her now! She looks as if she's been attacked by a plague of moths!' I wasn't sure what she meant but I looked gratefully at her because she is always loyal where I'm concerned.

'But she's disobedient,' the girl protested. 'I can't do anything with her.'

'I can see that,' U-M retorted. 'I think we'd better call it a day, don't you?' U-M reached for me and, having seen the girl off, got a pair of scissors and carefully clipped off the random tufts that had been left. There was nothing she could do about the bald patches but she cheered me up by saying, 'That looks better, Toffee, darling.'

Then she smiled. 'Don't worry. I'll find someone who is really good at dog trimming.' For the next few weeks I wouldn't have won a prize at Crufts but I was cool and comfortable and I'm not really conceited – as long as I'm clean, I'm happy.

Then U-M announced she was taking me to Purple Bone. Was it a nightclub for dogs? Would we be given purple-coloured cocktails and chicken canapés to nibble? Did she want me to mingle socially with other dogs?

When we arrived I saw a wonderful collection of toys . . . so was this place a day nursery? For a moment I felt alarmed as U-M handed me over to a girl who was sweet to me. But there was no need to worry. Elizabeth Arden and Estée Lauder eat your heart out! I was pampered by gentle hands and kind voices as I was clipped and had a lovely bath, then combed and brushed and blow-dried until I looked glamorous enough to strut along a red carpet, be it Buckingham Palace or the Oscars. They even sprayed me with a lovely perfume, so when U-M came to fetch me she said, 'You smell heavenly, Toffee.'

Do You Believe in Ghosts?

When the ghost of George appeared.

Of course I believe in ghosts, and so does U-M. Most animals have an extra sensory awareness of the spirit world that humans mostly lack. Nowadays people are so distracted by technology and material things that their awareness of spirituality has become blunted. Phew! That was a long sentence! Do you ever 'get a hunch' that something is going to happen . . . and then it does? And I don't mean knowing who is calling you when the phone rings. That's telepathy and quite different, and it happens to most people. I mean feeling shocked to the point of being ill for no reason, and then very shortly afterwards someone you know has died? That has happened to U-M and every time she thought she was coming down with flu and felt really awful, then *bang*! Someone she knows has suddenly passed away.

I'm told that the Queen's sporting Labradors who live at Sandringham know several days before she arrives, although their routine doesn't change, that she's on her way. It's the same with me and U-M. I know she's on her way home after a night on the town half an hour before she arrives.

I could write a whole book about the ghosts U-M and her family have seen. Buffy lived in a very haunted house at one point. He bumped into a nasty man in the hall one day and when U-M asked him what it was like, Buffy replied, 'It was like walking *through* someone.'

The drawing room was freezing even in summer, and I noticed U-M always gripped the banister because she feared someone would push her from behind down the stairs.

Many years ago when Baba and Buffy were small, U-M and Archie used to stay in a seaside cottage owned by her mother. Apparently even a spiritualist who kept in contact with dead people in their church every Sunday was terrified by whoever haunted the cottage. He shot out of his bedroom ashen-faced the first evening and said he couldn't sleep in that room. U-M went to sit in it to see if she felt anything and apparently she was very shaken, saying, 'It's as if there's an evil force that makes you want to run away, but I sat it out and it passed through me and faded away.'

I'm told there was a serious problem when Amber, their first Poodle, started growling ferociously as she watched someone walk across the room. Who had she seen? If only she could have talked, but there was no doubt she was frightened.

U-M and Archie bought a Ouija board and set it up on a table on its three legs with their tiny wheels and pencil and paper. God knows why, but they turned most of the lights off and placed their fingertips on the board, waiting to see what would happen.

'Stop pushing it!' U-M told Archie. He confessed he wasn't touching it. At which point I heard U-M tell a friend, 'The board started moving like mad although I wasn't touching it either. Then it stopped and I got a real shock. A message in my late grandmother's handwriting warned me never to stay at the cottage again.'

Some ghosts believe they're still alive. A priest who exorcises spirits told Buffy this interesting fact. Animal ghosts exist too. U-M had a friend to tea and they were talking about dogs, so I listened to every word. The friend, Jennifer, had spent a weekend with another friend at her country house.

'I walked into the dining room for breakfast and I saw sitting side by side on the stairs two Cavalier King Charles Spaniels,' she explained.

'I thought how sweet they looked, although there was something odd about their paws, and then I forgot about it until later.'

U–M was listening intently and so was I. Then Jennifer continued: 'I was talking to Clare later and told her I didn't know she had a couple of dogs. And she said to me, "You mean the two Cavalier King Charles Spaniels?" and I said "Yes". Clare smiled and said, "I've seen them too. I believe they lived in this house about a hundred years ago. Did you notice their feet looked, well, sort of not there?" I admitted I had.'

U–M was riveted and I was sitting with my tongue hanging out.

'What did Clare say?' U–M asked.

Then Jennifer explained that her friend had told her the staircase in the house had been rebuilt in 1934 and each step was now an inch or so higher than the original steps.

There was a silence, then U–M spoke slowly. 'So the ghostly dogs were standing on the original staircase. . .'

Well done! I thought. Go to the top of the class.

Only a few weeks ago Buffy had come home earlier than usual and walked up the stairs where U–M happened to be standing. Then he'd looked down at the floor with a puzzled expression.

'A cat just ran up the stairs with me,' he'd said.

'What colour was it?' she'd asked.

'Black.'

'Then that would be George,' she'd said calmly.

What the hell was going on? I hadn't seen anything but I knew George had been Buffy's cat, and he'd died about twenty-five years ago! Perhaps I don't have second sight? How disappointing.

Then U–M revealed that before I arrived and she'd been alone in the house with all the windows and doors locked, she'd woken up in the middle of the night and felt a cat high-stepping daintily up the bed behind her legs. The cat seemed about to settle in the small of her back, which George had often done. When she'd switched on the bedside light, she was alone.

What am I supposed to do if George appears again? Hopefully I'll sleep through his visitation. But he's not the only ghost in our house I've missed. Once, U–M awoke when she was ill in bed to find her late grandmother, to whom she was very close, standing by the bed and leaning over to see if she was alright. Then there was the occasion when she was sitting in our garden and she was sure it was me, sniffing under a very big hydrangea we've got, until

I came bounding out from the house into the garden. She said afterwards, 'I was so sure it was Toffee until Toffee appeared, so it can only have been Truffle.'

Well, we do look alike, so it makes sense.

How many more animal and human ghosts have I got to put up with? I haven't forgotten U–M comes from a big family and at one point she had seventeen pets . . .

A Lesson in Etiquette

Have you ever seen anyone raise their hand high above the head of another person in a gesture of greeting, before patting them?

Imagine a garden party on the beautiful lawn of Buckingham Palace with three thousand guests all raising their hands to . . . 'Woops! I do apologize, Your Majesty! I thought your face looked familiar!'

So why does everyone raise their hand over a dog's head? When it happens to me I wonder if I'm about to be hit, stroked or patted. We don't like it! The correct way to greet a dog is first to ask the owner's permission. Some dogs are aggressive and don't trust humans; others can be just plain scared.

If the owner indicates their dog has a friendly disposition, (like me) then you should offer the dog the palm of your hand, which should be held six to eight inches below the chin. Then the dog with his or her wonderful sense of smell will decide just how friendly we want to be. Is this person really a dog lover? Do they have a pet of their own? Or in my case do they want to suck-up to U-M?

People shouldn't think they can take liberties. We like to be respected. A gentle steady stroke of our backs or behind the ears is fine but anything more we consider to be abusive until we've made real friends with them. Nor are we deaf. If someone is flattering me in order to please U-M we can spot their insincerity in a flash. The nicest thing was said by a lady I would trust. Having talked to me for a few minutes, she finally said to U-M, 'She's a real little person, isn't she?'

I liked that. It was a very profound statement.

U-M had a friend to stay who did the unforgivable, because I think she was jealous that I preferred being with U-M. One day she grabbed me when I was in the garden minding my own business. She held me so tightly on her lap I couldn't move and she talked to me seductively, calling me a 'sweetie'. But I felt like a prisoner in her grip. As soon as U-M came into the garden I struggled harder than ever and looked at her beseechingly. I could see she didn't want to be rude either but she came up to us and said my name softly.

That was it! I made a superdog struggle to escape and managed to free my front legs, but she was still clutching my back half to her bosom. U-M looked concerned. She could see I was in danger of falling head first to the ground if the woman suddenly released me, so quick as a flash she bent down and actually caught me in mid-air. Then she placed me gently on the ground and I shot off. What I needed now was a drink!

I noticed the woman was very angry that I didn't like her but U-M was even angrier, although she didn't show it; but I noticed she was never invited again. The lesson is, don't mess with other people's dogs.

Another golden rule is never come up behind a sleeping dog to pat their back. The most good-natured dog in the world will wake up and in a nanosecond spin round to instinctively attack whoever has startled them. The motto is: *let sleeping dogs lie.*

U-M read aloud to Baba the story in a newspaper of a rescued dog who slept on the bed of his new owner. She was awakened in the middle of the night when the dog was having a nightmare and howling with terror. Instinctively she reached out to wake him but startled him instead and, still half asleep, he thought she was part of his dream. Whipping around, he bit off her nose.

When he realized what he'd done he fled down to the kitchen where he was found shivering with fear. The tragedy was he had to be put to sleep.

But what had happened to him in the past that caused him to react so violently? I'm sorry for the lady but I'd like the person who had obviously ill-treated him to be severely punished.

There are several lessons to be learned from this story.

The first is that you shouldn't sleep with someone you hardly know, be it an animal or another human.

The second is, please adopt abandoned dogs, but find out their background and then let them get to know you gradually to make sure you're compatible. You wouldn't marry a complete stranger, would you? Having a dog is a relationship for life, at least the whole of the dog's life. You can't divorce your dog because he's boring, can you? Or kick him out because he fancies a bitch?

When we go to stay with Baba and Rob on the Isle of Wight there are strict rules I must obey. If a ball is thrown for Millie I must let her win the race to get it, because that's only polite. She loves swimming and paddling in the river; but I like to keep my feet dry so I bask in a deck chair and let her get on with it. Don't get me wrong! I adore the countryside and the freedom of walking in the grounds for miles and miles without being on a lead. The thing is Millie can be popped into a bath to get rid of the mud, followed by a rub down with a towel, but if I had a bath and didn't have a blow-dry I'd start smelling like a damp cardigan and U-M would spend the whole weekend acting as my hairdresser.

The last etiquette tip is to send thank you letters. People really appreciate them. I'm thinking of getting one of U-M's portraits of me made into cards I can send to my fans. That would really increase my list of admirers, wouldn't it?

A Happy Christmas

I'm all lit-up! ~ like a Christmas Tree!

unp.
2010

Don't you just love Christmas? I adore it! All that wrapping paper to shred! All the presents piling up under the tree! All the family (over twenty in total) gathering in the house to see me and U-M and wish us a Happy Christmas, while the champagne flows and the mince pies and little sausages on sticks are handed around. U-M's grandson Archie loves those sausages so much he could hardly eat dinner that night. But not me. I don't want to get a 'middle-aged spread', whatever that is. My waist is as trim as when I was two, and that's because U-M watches what I eat like a hawk. I don't even know what human food is like apart from an egg scrambled with a little water. When I was only three months old I had a bit of a tummy upset and Mary Brotherton told U-M to give me that and it worked.

People who feed their dogs with the scraps from their plates are committing a real sin and shortening the lives of their dogs. One thing I never have is red meat, only chicken boiled in plain water. Added to that I am given raw grated carrots, and a little steamed broccoli is also good, laced with dry food and tinned chicken and rice, only available through the vet. Perhaps I'll write a cookery book for dogs. It could become a bestseller!

I do sometimes wonder why people gorge themselves with food over Christmas. Do they think famine is going to strike in the New Year? You see them stuff their faces and I find it disgusting. You'll be guilty of murdering your dog if you think giving him rich titbits is a treat they'll love. They won't thank you if they die of a heart attack when they could have had at least another two or three years of good health.

To get back to Christmas (why does food always dominate this celebration?), the greatest fun is helping Maria to decorate our house, from the wreath of green leaves and little white feathered birds on our front door, to garlands of glitter around the mirror in the hall. Then a big tree goes up in the drawing room, and it's hung with silver baubles, strings of silver beads and lots of fairy lights. There's usually a spangled fairy at the top, because I'm too big! I rearrange all the little decorations on the tables around the room but Maria then puts them out of my reach, so I'm left with the presents to arrange. Are there any for me? There probably will be because Baba always gives me something lovely and Maria gives me a toy animal which I take great care of, and keep safe under U-M's pillow.

One friend had the bright idea of giving me a collar with little blinking lights, so U-M could see where I was when she took me out at night. The very idea horrified me! I don't want to be winking and blinking like some cheap Oxford Street Christmas decoration! I barked a lot in protest and the friend seemed annoyed by my lack of gratitude and ended up giving me a pink rubber bone. Not quite my style, but as they say it's the thought that counts. One year Maria gave me a dark brown fur blanket to sleep on. It looks and feels like mink. Now *that's* what I call stylish.

I like it when U-M lights lots of scented candles, and you should see the dining room! She puts a white, lacy antique cloth on the long table then sprinkles it with handfuls of tiny silver stars. By the time she's placed the silver candlesticks and basket of tangerines, there's not much room for the food! Why does every place setting require three crystal glasses? Then there are piles of crackers that make a horrid noise when they're pulled, but I love dashing to pick up whatever falls out.

By now I'm curled up on U-M's lap and she's in good form quaffing wine and surrounded by her two children, her seven grand-children and (so far) her seven great-grandchildren, not to mention her in-laws. And, of course, she has me.

The English protest that they are a nation of animal lovers, but I really wish we lived in France where dogs are not only allowed into restaurants but are given a chair to sit on, and also a plate of what they'd ordered. They are treated like a proper member of the family. That's so civilized. U-M isn't allowed to take me anywhere, not even the bank or the post office. Otherwise I'd lunch at the Ritz with her, dine at the Dorchester, drop in to the Café de Paris and go shopping in Harrods.

What are people scared of? It's all to do with that rubbish about Health and Safety. We dogs are not going into a supermarket to have a pee and a poo! We're not going to spread some deadly virus among the population. It's a fact that there are more bacteria in a human's mouth than there are in a dog's. They've stamped out rabies and it's only herds of bovine that spread Mad Cow Disease.

U-M is very laid-back about all this. I can sit on her white brocade sofa as long as I haven't come back from the park with muddy feet. We share a double bed – I put my head on my pillow and she puts her head on hers.

Let's keep life simple, I say. We're not out to impress people, we're just ourselves getting on with our lives.

One elderly lady called me 'spoilt'. I strongly refute that. Making a child or a dog happy is not spoiling it. U-M tries to make Christmas as happy for everyone as she can, and that of course includes me.

I hope you have a very happy Christmas. You will if you have a companion like me to share it with.

The Way We Live

Our *modus operandi* is very simple.

I keep a constant eye on U-M to make sure she doesn't get up to any mischief. It means following her from room to room all over the house, but it's important to make sure she's OK. Supposing I hadn't been walking beside her when she fell and broke her hip? I made sure everyone knew it happened at 9.30 a.m.; I didn't want people to think she was drunk and disorderly in the evening. I supervised the ambulance men putting her on a stretcher and then Baba took over. When she finally came home Maria and I looked after her and made sure she had everything she needed. I took the night shift as Maria had to go home to her husband and daughters, and we soon had U-M up and about.

I wait outside the bathroom to give her a little privacy. I used to

sit and watch her having a shower, but as she likes to use a hand-
held shower and her aim is somewhat erratic, I used to get soaked
in spite of dodging around the room.

Rob said to U–M when I was very young, 'You can't let Toffee
rule your life.' Sensibly, she paid no attention.

There are different ways of ruling people's lives and if you're
helping to protect them from themselves, then it's a kindness. For
example, when U–M is entertaining I have to keep a close watch,
especially if there's a man around. The champagne flows and there
she is looking glamorous and flirting like mad. At some point I have
to get rid of him because I don't want a man, however nice, hanging
around the house and – horror of horrors! – suppose he wants to
sleep in our king-size bed? Where would I go?

When I think it's time he left I put my plan into action. I look
straight into U–M's eyes and give a little grunt. What it means is I
want to go out urgently. She smiles and strokes me but I'm not
giving up, and she knows it.

'What does Toffee want?' a man asked innocently one evening.
I grunt again – louder this time. U–M is aware that this is a ploy
because I went out earlier and I have a very strong bladder. Then
I can see U–M's got the message.

'I'm afraid you'll have to excuse me,' she says, rising and reaching
for my lead. 'Toffee needs me to take her out.'

It's an award-winning performance and only I know she's lying
through her teeth. The man offers to take me out. 'That's so kind,'
she replies, 'but I'm afraid Toffee won't do anything unless she knows
you very well.'

This is true. I'm a real lady and some things are private. He leaves.
Hooray! U–M has enjoyed a little chat and a drop of bubbly but
enough is enough. I think she's as happy as I am that we're on our
own again. We race up the stairs to our beautiful bedroom which
is large and airy and has two French windows leading on to a balcony.
U–M kicks off her shoes, flings herself in to a big armchair and
picks up the book she's reading while I lie by the open window
enjoying a gentle breeze which ruffles my coat when the weather's
hot.

Unfortunately she insists we shut the windows before we go to
sleep. I've told her I'm a brilliant watchdog; don't I bark whenever
someone comes to the door? I could sleep on the cool stone balcony
and cogitate on the absurdity of men. Not long ago one of her

friends accused *me* of being jealous because she was talking to him and not me.

We never argue, but she can be quite annoying at times. Why does she have to turn the bedding down an hour before we go to bed, which disturbs my evening nap? I can do it later. It only means pulling back the yellow brocade bedcover, and then I rearrange the pillows so beautifully.

In the winter I arrange the duvet into an igloo which is lovely and cosy. But when she gets into bed she straightens is out and adds insult to injury by calling me 'a funny little thing'.

I often have to tell her it's time for bed. There is just so much television I want to watch. I think *Big Brother* would be much more amusing if they filled the house with a dozen or so various breeds of dog!

Another annoying aspect is U-M's dinner parties. The first half hour is amusing with everyone arriving and making a fuss of me, and then I'll watch them getting merry on champagne. But the next two hours are a disaster. I can only see people from the waist down as they sit around the table and talk to each other! They've forgotten I exist. Even U-M talks nineteen to the dozen and completely ignores me. By the time I catch her eye I'm losing the will to live. How would you feel stuck under a plank of wood, surrounded by twelve pairs of feet which might kick you accidentally? I suppose I could go to another room but I don't trust U-M. Supposing she suggested they all go on to a nightclub? She loves to dance, but I don't trust her with men.

Then she'll move her chair back and, grinning, look down at me, saying, 'Hello Toffee.'

With one bound I'm on her lap, sitting up at the table like everyone else. The candles give a lovely light and, most importantly, I can be seen! There's always a little chorus of 'Toffee!'

Each time I just hope they don't stay too late.

As people go, U-M is fairly easy to live with. She only swears and gets angry with her computer, and she gives me my supper in the late afternoon, but I don't know why she takes me for a walk immediately afterwards. *Why?* I never need to do anything immediately after a feed. Do you? Does anyone right after they've eaten?

I stand at the top of the stairs and refuse to come down to the hall because I don't need to go out. I'll want to in a couple of hours but not right away. I know what's best and I still have a lot of things to teach her.

The first is: don't trick me! Once or twice she's lured me into a room with a biscuit . . . and then shut me in the room! She says it's for my own good to prevent me running out of the house if the front door is open.

I have to admit, she has a point. When I was very young I managed to slip past her and out of the house, where I ran up and down the pavement and even ventured round the corner, out of sight. U-M nearly had a heart attack. Then there was the time in Hyde Park when we were playing with a tennis ball which I decided I'd take home on my own. I trotted off and she was trying every trick to catch me, as there were two very busy main roads to cross to get back to our house. I was nearing the first road when I heard her yell to a couple, asking if they could catch me. I didn't want to be caught and tried to run past them but they succeeded in grabbing my collar. U-M put me back on the lead and she looked very pale. I was just having a bit of fun and wanted to put the ball under her pillow. When she tells the story she always adds, 'I had the most terrible migraine for the rest of the day.'

I suppose I am very spoilt, but I keep U-M company night and day and she makes me her first priority. When I think of all the dogs that are abandoned and how miserable they must be, I appreciate how lucky I am. Living with a kind and caring person is the best thing ever, and every dog deserves nothing less.

Lightning Source UK Ltd.
Milton Keynes UK
UKOW01n1826120416

272101UK00001B/2/P